Pinkie Pie's Party

Little, Brown and Company
Hachette Book Group
1290 Avenue of the Americas, New York, NY 10104
Visit us at LBYR.com
mylittlepony.com

First published as *Pinkie Pie and the Rockin' Ponypalooza Party!*
by Little, Brown and Company in July 2013;
Originally adapted in 2017 by Five Mile, an imprint of
Bonnier Publishing Australia in Australia.
First U.S. Edition: March 2019

Little, Brown and Company is a division of Hachette Book Group, Inc.
The Little, Brown name and logo are trademarks of Hachette Book Group, Inc.

The publisher is not responsible for websites (or their content)
that are not owned by the publisher.

Library of Congress Control Number: 2018946079

ISBNs: 978-0-316-48807-5 (pbk.), 978-0-316-48806-8 (ebook)

Printed in the United States of America

LSC-C

10 9 8 7 6 5 4 3 2 1

Pinkie Pie's Party

G. M. Berrow

LITTLE, BROWN AND COMPANY
NEW YORK ✳ BOSTON

Chapter 1

It is the first day of spring in Ponyville.
Gentle rays of sunshine make everything
sparkle.

"Wake up, Ponyville!" Pinkie Pie

calls from her bedroom window. "It's going to be an awesome day!

"I just love spring, Gummy!" Pinkie bounces around her pet alligator. "Smell this! It'll make you feel all flowery-powery!" Pinkie plucks a purple posy from her window box and holds it out to Gummy. The tiny gator chomps on the flower.

"Oh," says Pinkie. "Oh well." She trots across her room. "So, what's on the Pinkie Party Planner for today, Gummy?" She looks over the bright and colorful planner that Princess Twilight Sparkle gave her.

What Pinkie Pie sees horrifies her. No parties. Not one. There aren't any parties on today's schedule.

Pinkie's jaw drops.

"There's no way we can waste such a sunshiny day doing *nothing*, Gummy!" Pinkie grins. She has an idea!

"I know! We'll have a Spring–Sproing–
Spring Party to welcome the new season!
We have so much to do!" Pinkie bounces
out the door and into action.

Chapter 2

The center of Ponyville is the best spot to invite ponies to a party.

Pinkie Pie smiles at the crowd. "You're all invited to my Spring-Sproing-Spring

Party! This afternoon! By the lake! Be there if you like having fun!"

"A party? Can we come, Pinkie?" asks Apple Bloom. As usual, her two best friends, Scootaloo and Sweetie Belle, are by her side.

"Of course!" Pinkie shouts.

"Well, count the Cutie Mark Crusaders in," says Apple Bloom. "Maybe one of us will get our cutie mark while we're there!"

"I need you to help me out," Pinkie says. "Can you spread the word about

6

the party around Ponyville while I get

everything ready?"

"We'll do it!" say the Cutie Mark

Crusaders.

"Awesome!" Pinkie replies. "Okay."

Pinkie points to Sweetie Belle. "Start by

finding your sister."

Sweetie Belle nods and trots toward

the Carousel Boutique. Rarity is probably there right now, working on some new outfits.

"Scootaloo, you go to Rainbow Dash's cloud and tell her about the party so she can tell all of Cloudsdale!"

Scootaloo disappears in the distance, flitting her tiny wings.

"And you, Apple Bloom," Pinkie says, "are in charge of rounding up the entire Apple family!"

Apple Bloom sighs and scuffs the dirt

with her hoof. "Can't I go somewhere different than my house? Somewhere excitin'?"

"Good point, Apple Bloom," Pinkie Pie agrees. "Going to *new* places is way more fun! Why don't you take the path to Fluttershy's and stop at Twilight's on the way?"

"I'm on it!" Apple Bloom is off before Pinkie can say "Meet me by the lake!"

Pinkie Pie smiles. The party is going to be great!

Chapter 3

As Pinkie Pie bounces up the cobblestone path to Cheerilee's house, she notices something on the ground.

"I spy with my little Pinkie eye... something *SHINY*!" It is a rich red ruby!

"Come with me, little ruby!" Pinkie says to the stone. "I'll help you find your owner again."

Pinkie tries to pick it up, but the ruby just won't budge! Then she notices other sparkles across the ground. The path is dotted with gemstones! They look like rainbow sprinkles on a giant cupcake.

"Ooooh," coos Pinkie. "What a fun way to brighten up a front garden."

Just then, a mauve-colored pony opens the door. It's Cheerilee.

"Hiya!" says Pinkie, bouncing over.
"Your front path is like a party under
your hooves!"

"Thanks, Pinkie! They are garden
gems from the Crystal Empire."
Cheerilee smiles. "So, what brings you
here this morning?"

"You're invited to my first-ever,
totally awesome Spring-Sproing-
Spring Party!"

Cheerilee says with a chuckle, "I'll

be there. What would Ponyville do

without all your parties, Pinkie?"

Pinkie frowns. A Ponyville with no

parties sounds horrible!

"It would probably be really, really, really boring!" Pinkie says. "Bye, Cheerilee! Bring friends! Bring bouncy things!"

As the excited pony takes off, it's hard to tell which shines more—the pretty path or Pinkie Pie herself.

Chapter 4

The lake is beautifully decorated for the Spring-Sproing-Spring Party. Streamers and ribbons hang from the trees. Three pink trampolines are set up, along with a bouncy barn, jump ropes, and a bunny bed.

It is the springiest place in the land, and all the ponies are having fun trying out the many activities. They can't believe Pinkie Pie put all this together in just one day!

"She's so talented," Fluttershy says.

"*Wheeee!*" Pinkie Pie bounces up to her friends. "So, have you guys tried the bouncy barn yet?!"

Rarity sighs. "Oh, you know I normally

would, darling, except jumping and perfect hair do *not* go together!" She flicks her shiny purple mane and trots off to check out her reflection in the lake's surface.

"Pinkie, your Spring-Sproing-Spring Party is a smashing success," Twilight Sparkle says. "It seems as if the whole town is here! Even ponies I've never seen before. Like that group over there."

Twilight gestures over to where an older couple is standing with their two

daughters. They are frowning at the
festivities going on around them.

"I don't believe it!" Pinkie shouts.
She pulls out a glittery pink megaphone.
"Your attention, please! I'd like you all
to welcome to Ponyville ... my *FAMILY*!"

Pinkie throws confetti over the crowd and a cheer rings out. "That's my ma, Cloudy Quartz, and my pa, Igneous Rock! And two of my sisters—Marble Pie and Limestone Pie!"

"*They* are Pinkie Pie's family?" Spike asks Twilight. "But they don't look anything like her!"

"*Hmm.*" Twilight Sparkle looks thoughtful. "Well, families do come in all shapes, sizes, and colors."

Chapter 5

Pinkie Pie skips up happily. "Hi, Ma! Hey there, Pa! How's it going, Marble? What's new, Limestone? Are you here to party? I planned all this! Look, there are lots—"

"Pinkamena Diane Pie," Igneous
interrupts. "We are not here to party.
We are here for a very important reason.
We are here to see Her Royal Highness
Princess Twilight Sparkle about a very
urgent matter!"

Pinkie's face drops. "You're not here to party *or* to see me?"

"I'm sorry, but we have to talk to the princess and then get back to the farm right away," Cloudy replies. "We don't have time for any party nonsense."

"Oh," Pinkie says, sighing.

"It's not nonsense!" Twilight says, stepping forward. "And I'm right here." She uses her most regal voice. "Welcome to our fair Ponyville."

"Princess!" says Igneous with a bow.

"We would be so grateful if you'd help us out."

"I'll help in any way I can, Mr. Rock," Twilight Sparkle says. "Pinkie is one of my *very best friends*."

"That's great news, Your Royal Highness," says Igneous, taking off his hat. "You see…we are about to lose our rock farm."

"What?!" Pinkie Pie shouts.

"Oh, those poor little rocks," whispers Fluttershy.

"Say, Pinkie, are you okay?" asks Applejack, giving her friend a sideways glance.

Pinkie stands frozen to the spot. Her face is full of sadness. "It's time to go home," she says. "This party is...over."

Chapter 6

For the rest of the day, all Equestria is buzzing with chatter about how Pinkie Pie broke up a party!

Applejack leads Pinkie's family over to the big barn at Sweet Apple Acres.

"Come on inside, y'all," Applejack offers.

"What happened to the farm, Mr. Rock? And what can we in Ponyville do to help?" Twilight Sparkle asks.

"It's the gems!" Limestone blurts out.

"Ever since that Crystal Empire showed up again, all that's popular are stones that shine, sparkle, and shimmer!" Cloudy explains. Her bottom lip starts to wobble. "Plain old rocks are boring."

"No, they're not, Ma!" Pinkie cuts

in. "Rocks are so totally awesome! There's slate! And granite! And—"

"Well, tell that to the rest of Equestria," Marble Pie replies. "We haven't had any business for months!"

Now that Pinkie is thinking about it, it does seem as if a lot of ponies in Ponyville are really into jewels lately. Pinkie knows she has to do something—*anything*—to help her family! *Thinkie, Pinkie!* she says to herself. And then it comes to her.

"I know! I know! We'll throw a party!"

Pinkie shouts. "It will be ... a rock concert! We'll get bands to play and all types of rocks to decorate and invite all of Equestria!"

"I think ..." Igneous says, stepping forward. "That it's ..."

Pinkie's smile grows.

"It's ... the silliest idea I've ever heard in my life! This is not something one of your parties can fix. Why can't you be serious for once, Pinkamena?"

Pinkie's face falls. Usually fun can

help even the worst problems! All she wants to do is help. She makes a decision right then and there.

"I, Pinkamena Diane Pie, *Pinkie Promise* to be a super-serious daughter from now on and not to throw any more parties! Cross my heart, hope to fly, stick a cupcake in my eye!" With that, Pinkie's normally poufy mane falls flat and perfectly straight.

Pinkie Pie's friends all look at one another in complete shock.

Chapter 7

The next morning Pinkie Pie goes straight to work.

"No more messing around, Gummy!" she says. "I'm Pinkamena *Serious* Pie now. And I will find a super-serious way to save the rock farm!"

Pinkie rips down her Pinkie Party Planner and replaces it with a plain white calendar. Then she packs away all her party things. She has just started painting her room a boring shade of brown when she hears a knock on the door.

"*Oooooh*, a visitor!" Pinkie yells out, forgetting to be serious. It's Twilight Sparkle.

"*Hellooooo*, Twilight!" Pinkie sings

out. "I mean, welcome, Ms. Sparkle.

How may I help you this morning?"

Twilight makes a funny face. "So I

guess you *were* serious about being

serious, huh?"

"Abso-tootley-lutely!" chirps Pinkie, then she quickly corrects herself. "I mean. Yes, I am. I'm redecorating! Or should I say... *undecorating*? Once I fix this, finding a way to save the farm will be a piece of rock cake!"

"Brown paint? No parties?" Twilight asks. "Pinkie, this isn't who you are! We are going to plan the rock concert, just like you said! And we need your help."

"No thanks, Twilight!" Pinkie says, shaking her head. "You heard them....

My family isn't interested in my little parties. I have to find another way to save the farm."

Twilight trots to the door, feeling sad. "Well, Pinkie, I guess it looks as if *I'm* going to plan a rock concert. Let me know if you have any suggestions!"

Chapter 8

Twilight Sparkle has a collection of books on rocks, party planning, and rock music.

"Let's figure out exactly how Pinkie Pie does this," she says to her friends.

"I'm sorry, but how is studying rock books going to help us plan a rock concert?" Rainbow Dash asks.

"Maybe we should find some pony bands to perform at the show," offers Applejack.

"I could start on decorations," says Fluttershy.

Twilight closes the book. "You ponies are right. This isn't getting us anywhere."

"Where are the Pie sisters? Surely, they have some opinions on the matter," Rarity says. "It is *their* party, after all!"

"I doubt it," answers Twilight as she uses her magic to put away the stacks of books. Her Unicorn horn sparkles, and the books float gently up to their shelves. "If you haven't noticed, the Pies aren't too into parties."

"Where are they now?" wonders Fluttershy. "They looked so lost at the party yesterday."

Twilight nods. "I agree. That's why Spike is giving them a tour of Ponyville. I told them that Spike is my Royal Tour Guide and it is a special honor to be shown around by him."

"They sure do look up to ya, huh?"

Applejack comments, pointing to the tiara on Twilight's head.

"Now if only they'd believe me when I say the best pony for this job is Pinkie Pie!" exclaims Twilight.

"Don't worry," says Rainbow Dash. "Once we start putting the party together, Pinkie won't be able to help herself!"

Twilight looks at her party to-do list. "Rainbow Dash—you've just given me a great idea. I know exactly how to get Pinkie back!"

Chapter 9

Spike is showing the visitors all around Ponyville. Pinkie Pie's family certainly is starstruck by the royal pony. Cloudy wants to know Twilight Sparkle's opinion of every place they visit.

All of a sudden, Limestone and Marble gasp.

Cloudy yells out, "Iggy! Look over there!" They trot over to Cheerilee's house and look down at the gleaming, glittering gems.

"This is what's putting us out of business!" Cloudy cries. "And I hate to say it, but it does look nice."

Cloudy starts to cry. "We're doomed!"

Igneous hushes his wife. "Calm down, dear. We've got a princess on our side now! We'll all be back to work on the rock farm before you know it."

"Oh, you're right, dear. Thank Celestia that Pinkamena is stayin' out of it like a good lil' filly," says Cloudy.

Spike feels bad for Pinkie. She only wants to help! And now she is driving herself crazy trying to please her family.

Spike decides that the next stop on the tour has to be Sugarcube Corner. Maybe it will be just the thing to sweeten them up.

Chapter 10

Pinkie Pie has just finished changing all her bedroom accessories from bright, bold colors to shades of brown and gray when she hears a noise outside. Looking out the window she spies her family.

"Hey! Up *heeeeere*!" Pinkie is excited to show them how serious she can be. "This is where I live, family! Come up and see!" Pinkie shouts.

She turns to Gummy and giggles.

"Oh goody, goody rock hops! This is going to be fun! I mean—it's going to be … serious fun."

A moment later, Igneous, Cloudy, and Spike trot inside the colorless room. Pinkie does a little twirl.

"I undecorated! Just for you! Now I can be serious all the time!" Pinkie says.

"That's nice, dear. It's good to see you've made it look like the barn back home. Is that Granny Pie's quilt over there?" Igneous points to the gray-and-black blanket on Pinkie's bed.

"Oh yes, it is indeed," says Pinkie Pie. "Where are Marble and Limey? I want them to meet Gummy!"

Her pa says, "They are waiting

downstairs, Pinkamena. We don't have all day to just chat! We have business with the princess."

"Wait! You don't want to hear my serious ideas to save the farm?" Pinkie asks, looking crushed.

Cloudy pats Pinkie on the back before trotting out after her husband. "Tell us later, dear."

Pinkie's shoulders slump.

"Are you all right, Pinkie?" Spike asks. "Are

you sure you don't want to help Twilight and the girls with the party?"

There is a little glint in her eye, but it quickly passes.

"I'm totally fine-eriffic, Spike. No parties! Pinkie never breaks a Pinkie Promise, remember, silly? Gotta go! See ya later, Spike!" Pinkie Pie bounces out the door and down the stairs.

Chapter 11

Rainbow Dash and Applejack are standing outside Sugarcube Corner, holding a big bunch of balloons. All the balloons are misshapen or need more helium.

"Are you sure this is going to work?" asks Applejack.

"Of course it will!" says Rainbow Dash. "Pinkie will want to fix these balloons. Then, she'll be reminded of how much she wants to help with the party, and everything will be back to normal!"

"If you say so," Applejack says. "I just hope we didn't already miss her."

"Who?" asks Pinkie Pie, appearing next to them. She stares at the balloons.

"Applejack and I were put in charge

of balloons for the party," says Rainbow Dash. "These look perfect…*right*?"

"Yeah, they're, um…" Pinkie's eyes drop.

"Yeah?" says Applejack.

"They look guh-reat! Keep up the good work!" Pinkie says. "No time to stay and chat!"

Rainbow Dash turns to Applejack. "I thought we had her for sure!"

"Don't worry. The others are ready

to go," Applejack reminds her, watching Pinkie canter off into the distance.

As soon as Pinkie turns the corner by the Carousel Boutique, Rarity trots outside to catch her.

"Darling, I need your advice on the rock concert posters!" Rarity pulls out a large stack of hoof-made posters, each covered in pictures of flowers and bows.

Pinkie scrunches up her nose. "They're nice, Rarity, but why did you choose flowers and bows? It's a rock concert, silly!"

Rarity smiles. "Oh? What should I put on them?"

"Um...rock things?" Pinkie is itching to take over the party planning, but she remembers her promise to her family. "Actually," she says, "I think they are great like that. See ya later!"

Rarity sighs. "Well, I *tried*," she says to herself. "These posters are hideous!"

Chapter 12

Pinkie Pie is feeling funny. And not in a good way. She is starting to forget the reason she gave up parties. Pinkie finds herself imagining the right way to blow up a balloon and what kind of rock concert poster would look awesome.

When she arrives at the Castle of Friendship, Twilight Sparkle and Spike are there. So are Rarity, Applejack, Rainbow Dash, Fluttershy, and Pinkie's whole family!

"Is this a surprise party?!" Pinkie asks.

Then Pinkie remembers her serious plan. "I mean, not that I like parties. I hate parties!"

"You know that's not true, Pinkie Pie," says Twilight.

"Of course it is! I'm Pinkamena Serious Pie—the most serious-est pony in all of Ponyville!"

"We sure would like our old friend Pinkie back," Applejack says.

Rarity, Fluttershy, and Rainbow Dash nod in agreement.

"And we'd like our Pinkamena back, too," Igneous says, joining them.

"You...you would?" Pinkie can't

believe her ears. "But I thought that my parties were too silly for you! I thought you wanted me to be serious!"

"We're so sorry, Pinkamena, dear," Igneous says. "We didn't mean to hurt your feelin's."

Pinkie steps forward. "All I wanted to do was help!"

"We see that now, thanks to your friends here," says Igneous.

"We love you just as you are," Cloudy says.

Pinkie feels herself bubbling over with happiness. She runs over to her family and scoops up all four of them in a big hug. "You guys are the best!"

When she lets go of her family, her mane is at maximum poof. Pinkie Pie is back!

"Now that *that's* all over, we just have one question for you, Pinkie..." says Cloudy.

"What is it?!" Pinkie shouts, bouncing around. "Ask me! Ask *meeee*!"

Igneous clears his throat. "Will you plan our rock concert party?"

Pinkie pretends to think about it. "Oh, all right. If you really want me to!"

The group cheers loudly.

Chapter 13

Pinkie Pie bounces around the room, giving a job to everypony. It is all hooves on deck to rescue the party.

"Rainbow Dash, you're in charge of invitations!

"Fluttershy, you call your old pal Photo Finish and tell her to bring her famous friends! Spread the word that we need the biggest and rocking-est bands in Equestria to perform!

"Applejack! Ma!" Pinkie shouts. "You're next! You guys are in charge of *TREATS*! I want apples. I want rock cakes. I want apple rock cakes! Enough to feed all of Equestria! Go, go, go!

"Rarity! Twilight! Limestone Pie! Marble Pie!" Pinkie calls out. "You ponies

are in charge of...*DECORATIONS*!"
Marble and Limestone grin. Their
sister's excitement is catching on!

There is only one pony left with no
job. Igneous shuffles his hooves in the
corner. "What should I do, Pinkamena?"

"Pa!" Pinkie Pie bounces over to
him. "You have the most important job
of all!"

"I do?" he says. "What is it?"

Pinkie jumps into the air. "Have
fuuu-uuun, of course!"

Chapter 14

It seems as if all ponydom has come out for the party!

Pinkie Pie watches from Twilight Sparkles's hot-air balloon. "Welcome to *PONYPALOOZA!*" she yells into her

megaphone. "You're all going to have

the rocking-est time *EVER*!"

This is the biggest party Pinkie has

ever planned. And it's so awesome!

The entrance is decorated with

several large rock piles, bunches of

rock-shaped balloons, and a festive banner. There is a real buzz in the air.

Igneous Rock's eyes are wide with disbelief.

"How did little Pinkamena do all this? I've never seen so many ponies in my whole life!"

Twilight smiles. "You have a very special daughter. She sure knows how to bring ponies together."

She turns to Rarity and whispers, "Now, let's just hope it works!"

"Oh, it will, darling," says Rarity, winking. "It will!"

The two ponies hoof-bump. It is almost time to get this rock party started!

Chapter 15

Applejack is working the cider and apple rock cake booth. So far, the concertgoers are buying them faster than Applejack can dish them out!

Near the stage, Rainbow Dash is
pumping up the crowd with some
awesome Wonderbolt-style tricks. She
dives into a barrel roll and flies right
above the hundreds of ponies.

Then she lands on the stage and hoof-bumps a white pony with a blue-streaked mane wearing sunglasses. It is none other than DJ Pon-3, who is busy spinning some beats on her turntable.

The excited crowd stamp their hooves on the ground.

The sun is just starting to set over Ponyville as Pinkie Pie's balloon floats down onto the stage.

"Fillies and gentlecolts of Equestria!" Pinkie Pie shouts into her megaphone.

"I'm Pinkie Pie, and I'm here to welcome you to the first annual Pinkie Pie Family Rock Farm Ponypalooza Party!" The ponies go wild with cheers.

Pinkie bounces all over the stage. "Let me ask you this: Do you love rocks?! I know I do!" Pinkie screams into the megaphone.

The crowd starts chanting *rock* over and over.

"*Wahooooooo!* Are you ready to rock?!"

"Yeah!" the crowd yells back.

Chapter 16

The Pinkie Pie Family Rock Farm
Ponypalooza concert is a rockin' success!
Igneous and Cloudy are taking orders
for front path stones, cottage bricks,
and even pet rocks! It is incredible how

the rock farm has gone from struggling to thriving overnight.

"How can we ever thank you, Pinkie?" Igneous says. "You saved the farm!"

"I could never have done it without the help of my friends ... and you guys!" Pinkie Pie giggles. "Wasn't it a fantilly-astically great time?!"

"Abso-tootley-lutely!" answers her dad with a wink. "Be sure to come and visit us on the farm, now! Your mother's birthday is coming up really soon."

"A birthday?!" Pinkie's eyes grow wide. "You know what that calls for?"

"A party!" choruses her family.

"Hey! How'd you guys know what I was gonna say?!" asks Pinkie Pie.